BIONICLE®

CHALLENGE OF MATA NUI

BY GREG FARSHTEY

ILLUSTRATED BY
DAVE WHITE

SCHOLASTIC INC.

NEW YORK   TORONTO   LONDON   AUCKLAND

SYDNEY   MEXICO CITY   NEW DELHI   HONG KONG

ISBN-10: 0-545-16209-2
ISBN-13: 978-0-545-16209-8

12 11 10 9 8 7 6 5 4 3 2 1   9 10 11 12 13 14/0

Printed in the U.S.A.   23
First printing, November 2009

Mata Nui stood in the desert with his new friend, Ackar. They were on a dangerous journey to the village of Tajun. A traveler had to be prepared.

Ackar was an experienced fighter for the village of Vulcanus. He had won many battles in his life. But Mata Nui did not seem to know how to protect himself. Ackar decided to teach Mata Nui how to fight.

Today was the first day of class. Ackar wanted to take Mata Nui by surprise to show him that a good fighter always had to be ready. Ackar whirled his sword over his head. Then he brought it down toward Mata Nui.

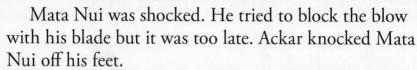

Mata Nui was shocked. He tried to block the blow with his blade but it was too late. Ackar knocked Mata Nui off his feet.

"Lesson one," said Ackar. "You have to know what your opponent is going to do before he does it."

Ackar helped Mata Nui get up. "How do I do that?" asked Mata Nui.

"You use your eyes and your brain," Ackar answered, smiling. "Now let's practice. Attack me with your sword."

"But what if I hurt you?" asked Mata Nui.

Ackar laughed. "You will have to hit me first."

Mata Nui swung his sword. Ackar blocked it easily. Mata Nui tried again . . . and again . . . and again. Ackar dodged or blocked his blow every time. Mata Nui started to wonder if Ackar was reading his mind!

When he was too tired to keep going, Mata Nui dropped his sword and sat down on the sand. "I need to rest," he said. "How do you do it?"

Ackar pointed at a huge bird with a long, sharp beak that was flying overhead. "Watch that bird for a minute."

Mata Nui did as he was told. The bird didn't do anything exciting. It just flew back and forth from its nest in the rocks.

"That bird is about to fly in a different direction," said Ackar. "Is it going to fly to the right or to the left?"

"How should I know?" asked Mata Nui. He was starting to get frustrated. What did bird-watching have to do with fighting?

"It's going to turn left," Ackar said. He sounded absolutely sure of it.

Mata Nui was amazed to see that Ackar was correct. The bird suddenly turned to the left and flew toward the sun. "That's incredible!" said Mata Nui. "You must know some fantastic trick!"

"We both watched the bird, but I watched closely," Ackar said. "Just before it turns, one of its wings flutters a little. Its right wing flutters before it turns to the right. Its left wing flutters before it flies to the left. By watching its wings, I can guess which way it is going to turn next."

Mata Nui smiled. "Okay. I am all set for a battle with birds, then."

Ackar laughed. "Keep watching. You will figure it out."

For the next hour, Mata Nui tried to predict how a creature would move. He paid attention to where it was looking before it jumped or flew or ran. He even listened to the noises it made. But nothing helped. Each time he made a guess, he was wrong.

"I will never be able to do this," Mata Nui said. He was tired of this game.

"Come with me," said Ackar.

He led Mata Nui across the sands and up into the rocks. When they were close to the top, Ackar suddenly stopped. He pointed to a strange creature up ahead.

"That's a rock steed," Ackar said. "It's one of the most dangerous creatures in all of Bara Magna."

It is certainly one of the strangest looking, Mata Nui thought. It stood on two legs and had two small arms. It had fierce jaws and a stinger tail like a scorpion. "It looks like a giant lizard," said Mata Nui.

"Giant lizards are nicer," said Ackar. "Get too close to a rock steed, and it will bite or sting you. But if you can tame one, you can ride it."

"How do you tame a creature like that?" asked Mata Nui.
"You need to win a fight against the animal," Ackar answered. "That's what I am going to do."

Ackar walked toward the rock steed. When the rock steed aw him, it hissed and snapped its jaws. Ackar moved to his ght. The rock steed watched him. Suddenly, the creature an at Ackar. It tried to bite him, but missed. Ackar grabbed e rock steed around the neck.

Mata Nui ran to help. Before he could reach Ackar, the rock steed attacked with its stinger. Ackar was hit! He fell on the ground. The rock steed looked down at him, ready to strike again.

"Hey! Over here!" Mata Nui yelled at the rock steed.

The creature turned from Ackar. It looked at Mata Nui and gave an angry hiss.

"That's right, big guy," said Mata Nui. The rock steed came toward him. That was what Mata Nui wanted — for it to move away from Ackar.

The rock steed struck at Mata Nui with its stinger tail. Caught by surprise, Mata Nui barely dodged the attack. Then the creature came at him with snapping jaws. Mata Nui jumped back to avoid being bitten.

"I don't know what's worse," said Mata Nui, "your sharp teeth or your bad breath."

The creature tried to sting Mata Nui again. Mata Nui almost fell off the mountain trying to avoid its tail.

"Okay, this isn't going well," he said. Mata Nui looked at Ackar, but the fighter was still not moving. Mata Nui knew his friend might be badly hurt. He had to end this fight quickly so he could help Ackar.

The creature came to attack Mata Nui once more. This time, Mata Nui watched very carefully. He saw the rock steed's right shoulder move a little bit. The next moment, the creature tried to hit Mata Nui's right side with its stinger.

"Now that's interesting," said Mata Nui.

He backed away from the creature. This time, the rock steed's left shoulder moved. Then the stinger lashed out at Mata Nui's left side. He was ready for it and batted it away with his sword.

"Okay, so if its right shoulder moves, it attacks to my right," said Mata Nui. "And if its left shoulder moves, it attacks to my left. Got it."

The rock steed came at him again. But this time, its stinger slapped against the ground. Then it lunged forward and tried to bite its enemy. Mata Nui was so taken by surprise that the rock steed almost got him.

"Stinger against the ground means a bite," Mata Nui said to himself. "Now let's see if I can use what I know."

Mata Nui got ready to fight. The rock steed charged. But each time it attacked, Mata Nui blocked it. It tried to sting and bite him, but it could never get Mata Nui.

The rock steed was really angry now. Mata Nui felt more confident with every passing moment. He knew he was ready for anything the rock steed might do.

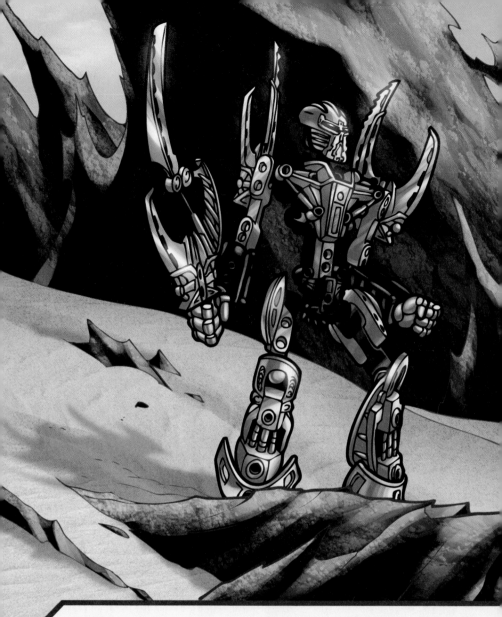

The creature came at him again. This time, Mata Nui smacked it with the flat of his sword. When the rock steed tried to sting him, Mata Nui struck it again. One step at a time, he drove the creature back. There was nothing it could do to stop him.

Finally, the rock steed gave up. With a loud hiss, it turned and ran away. Mata Nui watched it scramble down the slope and then run off into the desert. He had won.

Then Mata Nui heard an unexpected sound. Someone was clapping for him! Ackar was back on his feet and had not been hurt.

"I knew if you thought I was hurt, you would know what to do," said Ackar. "So I pretended the rock steed had beaten me. You thought my life depended on you winning."

"That was smart," said Mata Nui. "And I'm happy to see you are not hurt. But if you ever do something like that again . . . I'll push you right off this mountain!"

Ackar laughed. So did Mata Nui. Together, they made their way down the slope and back to the sands of Bara Magna.

Dear Family and Friends of New Readers,

Welcome to Scholastic Reader. We have taken more than eighty years of experience with teachers, parents, and children and put it into a program that is designed to match your child's interest and skills. Each Scholastic Reader is designed to support your child's efforts to learn how to read at every age and every stage.

- First Reader
- Preschool - Kindergarten GR
- ABC's   APR 1 9 2010
- First words

- Beginning Reader
- Preschool - Grade 1
- Sight words
- Words to sound out
- Simple sentences

- Developing Reader
- Grades 1 – 2
- New vocabulary
- Longer sentences

- Growing Reader
- Grades 1 – 3
- Reading for inspiration and information

On the back of every book, we have indicated the grade level, guided reading level, Lexile® level, and word count. You can use this information to find a book that is a good fit for your child.

For ideas about sharing books with your new reader, please visit www.scholastic.com. Enjoy helping your child learn to read and love to read!

Happy Reading!

—**Francie Alexander**
Chief Academic Officer
Scholastic Inc.

BIONICLE

Ackar must teach Mata Nui
how to fight. But when Ackar
is attacked by a rock steed,
Mata Nui faces a true test.

FIRST READER
LEVEL **PRE 1**
30-100 WORDS

ABC's &
first words.

BEGINNING READER
LEVEL **1**
50-250 WORDS

Sight words,
words to sound
out & simple
sentences.

DEVELOPING READER
LEVEL **2**
250-750 WORDS

New vocabulary
& longer
sentences.

GROWING READER
LEVEL **3**
700-1500 WORDS

Reading for
inspiration &
information.

Based on the best research about how children learn to
read, Scholastic Readers are developed under the
supervision of reading experts and are educator approved.

GROWING READER	GRADE LEVEL	GUIDED READING LEVEL	LEXILE® LEVEL	WORD COUNT
Level 3	1-3	O	520L	1392

"Scholastic Readers are designed to support your child's efforts to learn how
to read at every age and every stage. Enjoy helping your child learn to read
and love to read."
— Francie Alexander
CHIEF ACADEMIC OFFICER
SCHOLASTIC INC.

$3.99 US / $4.99 CA

LEGO **Based on the
LEGO® characters!**

ISBN-13: 978-0-545-16209-8
ISBN-10: 0-545-16209-2

50399

9 780545 162098
EAN

SCHOLASTIC

www.scholastic.com